The Old Apple Tree
and friends

By Jack Parnell

Copyright © 2020 Jack Parnell

All rights reserved. This book or any portion thereof may not be reproduced or used in any manner without the express written permission of the author except for the use of brief excerpts in a book review.

Illustrations by Lon Parnell & Bonnie Shields

Published in association with Keokee Books, Sandpoint, Idaho.

www.keokeebooks.com

Book design by Nicole Wolff, Keokee Books

ISBN 1-879268-56-4

First printing, 2020

PROLOGUE

I have had the desire for many years to say these things that are on my heart, in an effective and understandable way.

In the past I was given the opportunity to speak to very large crowds of thousands of people most of which were from an agricultural background like myself.

I have never felt that this message was reaching the right audience. While I know each was important, **I was preaching to the choir!**

Therefore, this book!

When asked by my publisher, "who is the audience?" I was taken by surprise! I had never thought about that. I wanted to write another book for kids, with content that adults must understand as well! How can it be interesting for both?

So, this is my attempt to say what I wanted to say and hopefully in a way that will make it fun and interesting for both.

I send this book out with the prayer that at least a few people (a lot of kids) will enjoy and have their hearts and minds opened and stimulated with some interesting ideas, both those who read and those who are read to.

CHAPTER 1

I'm starting this story with my personal history to hopefully set the stage for an extremely exciting and **thought-provoking** journey...

I was a typical farm boy born in 1935 and raised on my father's dairy in Fair Oaks, California.

Our dairy was small, even in those days, but through my young eyes it was **Gigantic**. This was in the early 1940's and the second World War was still raging on, so things were considerably different then. Squadrons of airplanes flying overhead, Air-raid warning sirens were going off each day, the protective blimps were flying over the Bay Area to protect against a possible attack and necessary goods were in short supply.

For instance, when you needed certain things like new shoes, we shopped for them at a store called "the Cash Mercantile." We used a war-time script called "Ration Stamps" along with money to pay. They were most important and that made money secondary!

In my family I had a dad, a mom, one brother and two sisters. We worked **very Hard** as each of us had a lot to be accomplished every day.

A typical day for me went like this:

Get to the barn and get it ready for morning milking, which meant **Everything** had to be **Squeaky Clean**. Next, we got the cows in and washed them down, so they were ready for Dad to begin milking at precisely **4 a.m.** Then the bottling of the milk began. Because we sold milk to the public it went into special tall glass bottles and we delivered them right to our customers' homes!

So, while the cows were being milked, we bottled it up after it ran over a special cooler. We did this all over again at **4 p.m.** You see, cows need to be milked two times each day. We also had the bottles from the day **before** to wash and sterilize! After that, we had to tend to the chickens, feed the calves – we grew our own "replacement heifers," fixed the fence if need be and cared for the garden. **ALL** of this was repeated the next day.

I loved the cows and milking time was my favorite time! I could hardly wait to take the old tin cup and sample the fresh milk as it came cascading, ice cold, over the cooler.

CHAPTER 2

As a very young boy I can remember being amazed and impressed at how Mother Earth was so free with her Gifts to us! We were poor by most standards, but we had an abundance of food on our farm. Lots of fresh milk, butter and cream, vegetables from our garden, fruit from our trees, meat from our cattle and pigs and tons of eggs from our chickens.

I was fascinated by our tomato vines. **So many tomatoes!** Our carrots, beets, turnips, lettuce, cabbage and potatoes all produced more than we could ever use, so we shared with our neighbors! It seemed to this farm boy to be **Nature's Magic!**

I loved the dairy cows but as far back as I can remember, I have had a love for Angus cattle and after what seemed to me to be **an eternity of wishing and dreaming,** the day came! She was a surprise gift from my parents! Her name was "Ellen Eris of Ebony" and she was a beautiful Angus heifer. When I saw her, I cried with tears of joy! Every day I would halter her and walk out among the giant Oak trees in our bottom field where the Spring grass was tall and lush. She would happily munch on grass while I marveled at those giant trees and day-dreamed,

"If only they could talk! They've lived so long! They must be wise!"

I would silently think to myself,

"I wonder what they would say?"

CHAPTER 3

Now that I am much older, **a lot of water has run under this bridge,** I continue to have a great fascination for trees, their beauty, their importance, their magnificence and over the years that feeling has grown much stronger!

Well, enough about me! That was then and this is now!

Today, we live on a beautiful ranch in Sandpoint, Idaho. We love and raise Clydesdale horses. I continue to have a lot of jobs to do! I fix fences. I put round bales out, harrow the pastures and in the Summer and Fall months, mow the pastures. **It's a lot of fun, but I am older, slower** and **get tired more easily!**

Around noontime, I am looking for the shade of a friendly tree to sit down under and eat my lunch and maybe even take a short nap!

"...ZZZZZZ"

My favorite tree on our ranch is a very old apple tree. She spreads her branches freely but though her trunk is gnarled with age, she provides a perfect resting place and a lot of shade for a rest!

CHAPTER 4

On this particular Fall day, I had started to mow pastures very early in the morning and around noon time, I was more than ready for lunch and a break. I sat down under that old apple tree, leaned up against her old gnarly trunk, took a bite of my peanut butter and apple jelly sandwich and as I did so, memories of my youth filled with Angus heifers, huge Oak trees and grassy meadows began to flood through my mind. As I relaxed, I thought to myself, "**This old apple tree has seen so much. I bet she is very wise; I wish she could talk!**" I wondered what she would say!

Some time went by, I can't know how much, when suddenly, as if by magic, she cleared her throat and began to speak to me!

Was this a dream? Was this real?

As she began to talk, her voice was very soft but confident. She thanked me and said she had waited many years for just the right time to have this conversation with me.

After a short pause she continued...

"I have something very important to share with you!"

She seemed very happy!

"**But first,** let me tell you where I came from..."

CHAPTER 5

"I was planted many, many years ago when the early settlers first came to North Idaho.

They brought the **seed** that I came from.

They planted it and with very tender and loving care and grafting

I Became Big And Strong!

Many winters have come and gone, and many very special people have enjoyed my fruit and have cared for me. So, I feel very blessed to still be here and to have this opportunity to share with you."

"Hmmmm, where do I start?" she questioned.

After a thoughtful pause she continued.

"Can you imagine how many apple pies have been enjoyed because someone planted and cared for a seed so many years ago?"

Before I could answer she continued.

"Please, forgive me. But let me digress for a moment, I have something **Very** interesting and fun to share with you," she said apologetically.

"In the early days the women from all the neighboring farms came over in their horse-drawn buggies. **Boy were they a sight to see!** They came to prepare for the Fall Family Get-Together Dinner and Dance. They also combined it with their Annual Pie Baking Contest and **wow!**"

"I can almost smell those pies now!

The entire neighborhood showed up. They all came prepared to cook and bake wearing their handmade flowery aprons made from old feed sacks. What a great sight it was! It was the highlight of the year, and was held in that old barn, right over there."

She took a deep breath and thought for a while as if she was silently enjoying her memories and then she continued...

"The baking contest was a serious competition but always very friendly," she said with a smile in her voice.

"Always lots of fun! The kids would dunk for apples, skip rope, shoot marbles and play Hopscotch. They wouldn't dare interrupt their mothers during the baking contest! What great times they had!" she exclaimed.

"After the pie baking was done and the sun was setting over Schweitzer Mountain the men would start to appear after a hard day's work on their farms. Some farmed the land, some were loggers, some were teamsters and…

They Were All Hungry!

They would wash up, put on a clean shirt and join the festivities. The wonderful smell of smoke from the old wood stove filled the air and as the women prepared for dinner, the men sat nearby playing their fiddles, plunking on their old guitars and playing 'The Spoons'."

"Whew! This is bringing back great memories!" she said with a sigh. "The smell of bread dough rising in the warming-oven, then the smell of freshly baked bread!

The kids replenished the wood box for the old woodstove. But as they did, there was a frequent caution from the mothers to 'not make a ruckus around the stove!' or... 'the rising bread may fall!'"

"The menu for dinner was usually wild turkey and grouse. Lots of potatoes and gravy. Carrots, onions and sweet potatoes smothered in marshmallows and brown sugar...and homemade bread!

Then the dinner bell rang!

After the blessing, thanking God for the abundance of delicious food, they ate.

Oh, How They Ate!"

she said as though her stomach was full.

"Not long after dinner, the ice cream freezers came out. The kids would go to the ice shed for ice and then a short trip across the field to Poelstra's Dairy for eggs and cream. Then the churning began! Vanilla in one, chocolate in another and fresh sliced apples in yet another. It didn't take long for the complaining to begin, **'Will This Ever Be Done? My Arm Is Tired!'** Each child took their turn in that very long process!

The youngsters got a great workout!" she exclaimed.

"Finally finished with the churning of the ice cream, the pies were cut into generous pieces and the ice cream in abundance, covered each slice! They all ate until I thought they would explode!

Then the men all judged the pies!

There was complete silence.

Finally, the announcement came that the winner of the pie baking contest was..."

'Everyone!'

"They each received a blue ribbon!"

"After a giant applause, away they went, up into the loft of the old barn for the dance. What fun," she remembered.

CHAPTER 6

She seemed very deep in thought as she spoke...

"The next day, when the festivities were over, all of the women would return to clean up and to 'Can' or 'Put Up', as they called it, applesauce to help feed their families through the long winter. A couple of women would pick, a couple of women would peel and slice, while the others prepared the jars in hot water over an even hotter wood stove. When the applesauce was finished there was enough for every family. Then the fruit press would come out of the basement to use up the remaining apples —apple juice for all!" she exclaimed.

"They didn't waste an apple! Can you even guess how many apples have been plucked from my branches? Or how many people I have fed?"

I was silent. I didn't try to answer her!

"In those early days most people grew their own food. Today, a small percentage of our people grow food **or Even Know How!** These days it is very easy to take our abundance of food for granted!" she said sadly. "Sorry," she added, "I'm getting way ahead of what I wanted to say!"

CHAPTER 7

After collecting her thoughts, she sounded excited.

"These days, I get great joy when it's harvest time and Michelle insists that all of my fruit is picked and placed in baskets to be shared with all of her neighbors or made into applesauce or cider or maybe even shared with the horses!"

Now a pause in her voice, then she continued.

"Michelle has great respect for that **SEED that was planted so many years ago!** And my goodness, you should see her garden!

Are You Listening?" she inquired politely. I assured her that I was!

Before I get to what I really want to talk about, I want to explain to you all that I do!

Providing you with apples is just the 'Tip Of The Iceberg.'

Pay attention now," she scolded. "This is very important!"

"Shhhhh, you must promise not to tell a soul.

Promise?" she asked.

I promised!

"I secretly drop apples from my branches very early in the year so that the momma deer with baby fawns can get the fresh food they need. They come in the early morning to see what I have dropped for them. Then, they return in the nighttime to avoid danger to see if there were any apples that they missed. I truly love them," she said. "They are my friends."

CHAPTER 8

This fabulous new tree friend of mine continued to talk as I listened intently.

I was speechless!

"Thousands of birds come to rest in my branches every year and sometimes they can't resist pecking at my tasty fruit. Some build their nests in my branches and stay all Spring to hatch their babies in the safety of my highest limbs.

Beautiful babies. I love that time of year!" she said with excitement in her voice.

"I even have a perfect hole in my trunk that provides a special home each season for regular visitors!"

"From time to time I get visits from my friends Mr. and Mrs. Bald Eagle seeking a resting place after their morning hunt. They rest a while, then fly on.

They are beautiful **but very heavy!**" she groaned.

CHAPTER 9

With greater enthusiasm, she continued...

"Oh boy! Oh boy! OH BOY! Wow WEEE! You should see the thousands, maybe millions of honeybees that visit during my blossom time! They collect the nectar from my beautiful flowers then fly away to their home to make honey to feed themselves and a lot of hungry people who love Apple Blossom Honey!

Oh my! I can almost taste it now!"

She continued:

"I see lots of Hummingbirds as they go about their migration. They dart from one place to another displaying their extreme beauty, then disappear.

It must be fun to fly like that," she speculated.

CHAPTER 10

She sounded exuberant now as she spoke again in a very loving tone, "Do you remember the book, **My Name is Ramsey: I'm A Clydesdale Stallion**? He was my very Special Friend. **The Clydesdales, Ramsey** and **Protege** and **all their daughters**, love my apples and it makes me very happy to hear them chewing with great enthusiasm. They sound like your grandma's old washing machine!"

She continued to talk but in a more serious voice now...

"I love the wind in the Selle Valley, she is my very special friend. I wave my branches as she passes by. Where has she been? Where is she going?"

"She touches me and we make beautiful music as she whistles through my branches. She then continues her journey. I love her!

I wonder to myself, 'When will she be back?'"

CHAPTER 11

"Elk and bear drop by for a brief visit on occasion. But, never together! They snack on my delicious fruit then continue on their way. I even see a pesky raccoon from time to time. They are cute," she observed. "Wild turkeys with their new brood of chicks will often search for a snack of fresh apples in the shade of my branches. What fun I have with all of my friends!" her voice showed great affection!

CHAPTER 12

"Oh! I almost forgot!" she exclaimed. "One of my favorite times is when the barn kittens come to play among my branches. They romp and play and box each other as they run up and down my trunk. **Sometimes, I fear that they will fall.** Many days, Clyde, the ranch Border Collie, will come down from the main house to pay his respects. He jumps and barks and snaps at the air. They all bring me great joy!"

She became very quiet and began to speak in a very serious tone...

"Just think!

All of this has happened because someone had the forethought to plant

and care for a single seed

That Became Me!"

CHAPTER 13

"So, you can see that I do a lot more than just grow apples. There are so many things that I would like to share in such a short time, so I better get on with the most important thing that I have observed over my many years."

She became very serious and I was listening intently.

"Did you know that in each one of my apples there is amazing **Power?** In each apple there are six to eight seeds. If properly cared for and fertilized, each seed has the power to become a tree.

Are you paying attention?" she asked sternly. "This gets pretty tricky."

I responded, "**I am!**"

"Well then", she said. "Let's see, each apple has, let's say...

six seeds and we know it takes about six apples to make a pie.

The apples in that pie would have a total of thirty-six seeds. Each seed, if properly cared for, could make a tree and each tree can produce five-hundred apples per year and live thirty years!

"**Wow!**" I thought.

"Maybe, the important question is **Not** how many seeds are in an apple...

But How Many Apples In A Seed?"

"Do you understand what I am saying?" she asked.

"**Unbelievable!**" I thought... or dreamed.

"You figure it out," she exclaimed. "I'll give you a hint:

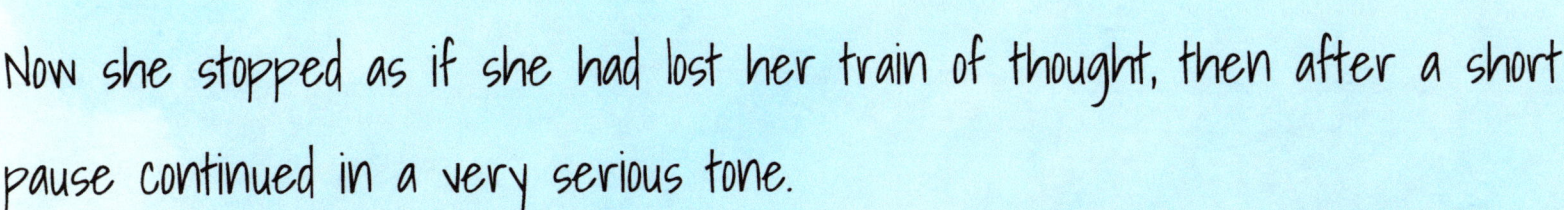

It Is Our Great Creator At Work!"

Now she stopped as if she had lost her train of thought, then after a short pause continued in a very serious tone.

"Apples are only one of God's great Creations. All seeds are powerful and magic. One kernel of corn planted and cared for will produce a stalk with two ears of corn, each of which will have six-hundred kernels on it! Aren't you amazed?" She asked.

She was so enthusiastic that she continued before I could answer!

"Just think, an almond tree will produce fifty pounds of almonds each year for over fifty years. Wow! A peach tree will produce sixty to sixty-five pounds of peaches each year for many years and, pay attention now..."

"They both grew from a single seed.

Isn't that exciting?" she asked.

"Think with me now. Concentrate! Isn't this where **much** of our food comes from?

SEEDS!"

I remained silent as she continued.

"Tomato plants can produce fifty to eighty pounds of tomatoes each year and it grew from a single seed so small you can barely see it. More magic!

All in God's perfect Plan!" she said reverently.

She pressed on in that very serious tone...

"Because so few people grow the food that the world consumes (less than 2%) we have become **very complacent** and **take it all for granted.** Just recognize that our farmers are so efficient that food is cheaper in the United States than anywhere else in the world. Less than 10% of our disposable income is spent on food. That leaves families money for new cars, TVs, cell phones and video games and it can be accomplished year after year because a farmer planted **a single seed.**

Farmers Are True Unsung Heroes!"

Sternly she asked, "Did you know, when you go out to dinner, the 20% tip that you leave the waitress or waiter is **More Money** than the farmer was given who grew the food that you had just eaten? Think about that!" she said with a demanding tone to her voice.

She seemed sad as she continued...

"I have heard some say,

'I hear what you are saying but I am not in Agriculture, I have no interest in it. It doesn't affect ME!'

If you eat, you **are!** And it **does!**"

"So, please, please, please, think about this," she said "and appreciate it and be thankful for **Farmers, Seeds** and your **Food**."

CHAPTER 14

Her voice became very measured as she continued to speak.

"There are many things that I would like to share. Perhaps the most important thing that I have come to know is that our Creator has planted **Seeds of Greatness in every child that is born.**"

"**Read Psalms 139:** He knew us before we were born as we were being formed in the darkness of our mother's womb.

They must be tenderly cared for, developed and cultivated just like an apple seed!"

She continued with love in her voice,

"Each child will travel this road that we call life. Many of you can walk on it **with them, But No One Can Walk On It For Them. They will need loving instruction.**

Teach them that they should be quick to listen, slow to speak and slow to anger!"

They will be born male or female without choice, but they will become **ladies** or **gentlemen** as a matter of how well those God Given seeds are cared for! Do you see my point?" she asked with great affection in her voice.

I did, but did not answer.

"Teach them that if they don't ask questions, they will **never** get answers.

If they don't **step forward**, they will **always** be in the same place.

Teach them that there is no harm in losing. But there is harm in never running the race!

Nurture those Seeds."

CHAPTER 15

She began to speak now in a voice that seemed to be very thoughtful and urgent.

"Before you go back to work, I feel obligated to reiterate a couple of thoughts.

God, during Creation, has given Mother Earth the ability to feed the world. Each plant produces its own seeds. Each can reproduce itself. Thousands of times over and over again! Taking nothing out in the process and feed us with abundance!"

"Even more important, it is a miracle of our Creator that each child is born into this world with seeds of Greatness. However, like plants, they require cultivation, love and teaching. But above all, lots and lots of love.

Let's not forget either," she urged, "it all starts with a small seed. Care for it!"

I felt she was about to say goodbye, when suddenly she exclaimed,

"Oh wait another seed for thought," she offered with a chuckle in her voice.

"Pardon the pun.

You no doubt notice that everything I do is for...

Someone Else."

"Maybe, just maybe as you nurture these young people in your life you could teach them that **Only They** have control over their thoughts and feelings and **Only They** have control over their actions. So, impress upon them that when they get up each morning they should ask themselves the question:

'What can I do for someone else today?'

You know, I strongly believe the world would become a much, much better place."

CHAPTER 16

"Oh, my goodness!" she said with surprise in her voice.

"I see that you are moving around and stretching. I'll bet you need to go back to work! I have waited so long to have this conversation; I can hardly stop talking! I have really enjoyed our time together!" she said in a very serious tone.

"Oh! One last thought," she said.

"Remember to be thankful each day for two things:

Our abundant food supply and 'our kids,'
They are our greatest natural resource!"

"Oh my!" she exclaimed as she began to yawn. "Now I am getting a bit weary myself! As you can see, I have worked very hard this year and as you may have noticed my leaves are flying away with my special friend The Wind."

"I will soon go to sleep and wake up in early Spring when my nap is over to do my job and greet my many friends once again! Oh, by the way,

I will be eagerly waiting for you to come by and chat again!"

CHAPTER 17

I woke up with a start! My head was spinning with thoughts of this magical conversation. I seemed to have a brand-new appreciation for this beautiful ranch and all the plants and trees that grow on it. The thought occurred to me that we live in the midst of a very special part of **God's Creation**. I also noticed that I was having significant thoughts about my responsibility to help nurture and love on those precious kids that come my way. The words of my **Special Friend** the Old Apple Tree continued to ring in my ears,

"Take care of those Seeds."

I went back to mowing our pastures, but I must confess...

I can't wait until spring!

the end.

PHOTO GALLERY

This is me, Jack with my lovely wife Michelle. I spent my entire life in agriculture, starting on my father's small dairy. I have served as Secretary of Agriculture for the State of California, as well as Deputy Secretary of Agriculture, and acting Secretary of Agriculture for the USA under President George H.W. Bush. Michelle has a lifetime love for horses and is in charge of our breeding program. She is a very talented horse person and my best friend.

This is a photo of the old apple tree with a set of fawns enjoying the apples that were dropped on the ground from her branches.

Clyde the dog and our cat playing around the old apple tree.

My wife Michelle driving her favorite Clydesdale.

We're so blessed to have the opportunity to nurture these little "seeds". (A few of our Grandchildren).

This is a young tree that my son Will and his daughter are helping to cultivate. Trees need water and sunlight!

We're a Clydesdale Farm. We breed and raise Clydesdale horses.

This is me with my cat on the farm. He's watching me as I do business over the phone.

My granddaughter Kinley, feeding one of our horses Ramsey. Ramsey loves apples!

This is my Grandson Jack. Ramsey also loves carrots!

This is our beautiful farm in Sandpoint Idaho. It gets cold here in the winter. Look at the beautiful snow!

This is our farm in the summer time.

Here are our hourses bringing in the sleigh to the barn for the evening. Working on a farm is hard work, but so rewarding!

Here are more pictures of the farm. **Above:** Out my window, the cat says hello!
Top right photos: These are photos of Protegié and Ramsey. **Bottom right:** This is a milk bottle from the farm I spoke about in the beginning of the book. My father owned Parnell's Dairy, It's the dairy that I grew up on in Fair Oaks California.

A SPECIAL THANKS

I will never be able to find words adequate to express my appreciation for all the people who helped make this book possible.

First to my wife Michelle who was very understanding of my time and always willing to help. To Dee Radermacher who typed and changed numerous editions, to Lon Parnell for his great art, and to Bonnie Shields, or as I call her "among the very best artists in the country."

I also want to thank my entire family who gave me strength of conviction and the will to stick to my belief in God and His abundant agriculture.

This is Dianna, also known as "Dee". She grew up in Sandpoint, Idaho. As a young kid and into her teen years she participated in Horse and Sheep 4H. During her senior year of high school, she represented Idaho State as its Draft Horse Queen. Some of her fondest memories are summers spent showing Belgian draft horses and haying with those same horses on Dover Ranch, just outside Sandpoint. She is a photographer now and has contributed to the annual Budweiser Clydesdales company calendar for five consecutive years. Dee is married to one of the drivers for the West Coast Budweiser Clydesdales hitch and they have one son who is also married and is working towards being a crop duster. Thank you Dee for all your help with this book!

ENDORSEMENTS

Pam Minick
RFDTV
Gentle Giants

" I love the life lessons and connection to nature in *The Old Apple Tree*. Jack Parnell reminds us that there is beauty all around us! The perfect family read and a great follow up on *My Name Is Ramsey*"

Jack Block

Secretary of Agriculture

President Reagan

"I compliment you on your creativity. It reminds me of my childhood growing up on a farm loving Angus cattle.

Using your old apple tree to tell the story is something many of us can relate to. We picked apples form our tree and made apple pie and churned our own ice cream.

Your book will be a learning experience for kids but also for gown ups... [I'm] Not sure we all appreciate the abundance that we have, through God's creation. It is truly our responsibility to nurture and protect these resources."

"It is very fitting that this book is written by someone who has dedicated a major portion of his life serving agriculture. Great book for parents or children."

Jim Herbert
Founder & CEO
Neogen Corporation

Printed in the USA
CPSIA information can be obtained
at www.ICGtesting.com
LVHW060830081023
760263LV00082B/306